This item must be returned or renewed on or before the latest date shown

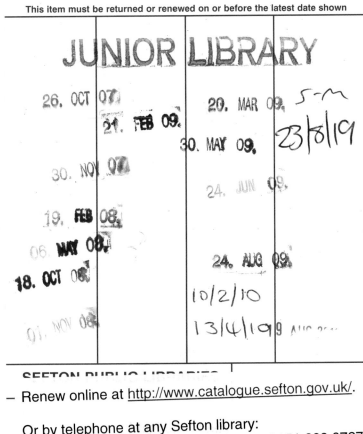

JUNIOR LIBRARY

26. OCT 07

21. FEB 09

30. NOV 07

19. FEB 08

06. MAY 08

18. OCT 08

01. NOV 08

20. MAR 09 5-m

30. MAY 09 23/8/19

24. JUN 09

24. AUG 09

10/2/10

13/4/19 9 AUG 2...

SEFTON PUBLIC LIBRARIES

— Renew online at http://www.catalogue.sefton.gov.uk/.

Or by telephone at any Sefton library:
— Bootle: 0151 934 5781   Meadows: 0151 288 6727

Crosby: 0151 257 6400   Netherton: 0151 525 0607

Formby: 01704 874177   Southport: 0151 934 2118

A fine will be charged on any overdue item plus the cost of reminders sent

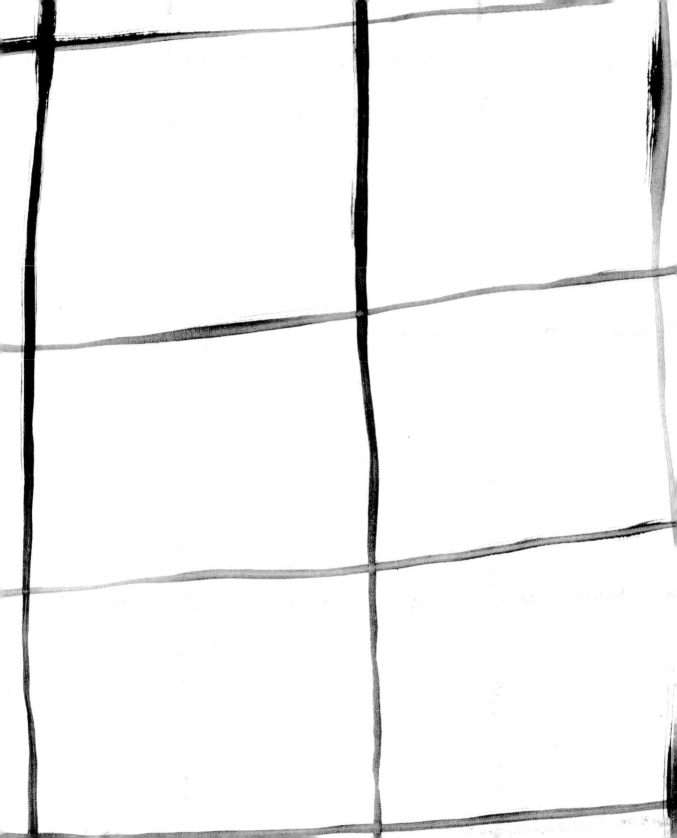

First published in Great Britain in 2007
by Zero to Ten Limited
2A Portman Mansions, Chiltern Street,
London W1U 6NR

This edition © 2007 Zero to Ten Limited
© Gallimard Jeunesse 2006

First published in France in 2006 as
Rita et Machin à l'école

All rights reserved. No part of this publication may be
reproduced or utilised in any form or by any means,
electronic or mechanical, including photocopying,
recording or by any information retrieval system,
without the prior written permission of the publisher.

British Library Cataloguing in Publication Data
Arrou-Vignod, Jean Philippe, 1958-
Rita and Whatsit at school
1. Rita (fictitious character: Arrou-Vignod) - Juvenile
fiction 2. Whatsit (fictitious character) - Juvenile
fiction 3. Schools - Juvenile fiction 4. Children's stories
I. Title
843.9'54[J]

ISBN 9781840895124

Printed in China

JEAN-PHILIPPE ARROU-VIGNOD ❋ OLIVIER TALLEC

Rita and Whatsit at School

ZERO TO TEN

The teacher said no one was allowed to take soft toys to school.
'Hmm,' thinks Rita.

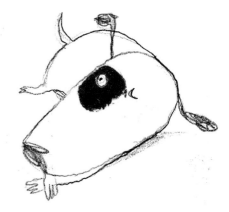

'Well,' says Rita, 'you are not a toy,
you are a real dog. I've got an idea…'

When Rita gets to school the next morning, no
one notices anything odd.
Her friends don't spot anything, and nor does
the teacher.
'No fidgeting,' Rita whispers.
'And hide your nose, or the game is up!'

It's very dark in Rita's
school bag.
Her break time snack smells
very tasty.
So do her dance shoes, and
those half-chewed sweets.

Whatsit is quite happy to take a little nap…

In class, it's painting time.
Rita tries hard not to go over the edge.

Suddenly…

'Miss! Someone has messed up
my painting!'

Now it's time for gym.

Rita and her friends go for the record in building the
highest human pyramid, when suddenly…

'Miss! Someone pushed me!'

Rita is in the lunch hall.
On the menu are all her favourites –
pasta and peas and peaches.

But suddenly…

'Miss! Someone's pinched food
from my plate!'

'Hello Whatsit. You've
been so good!'

'I've brought you a treat. But
remember – hide your nose!'

In the classroom, not a sound. Everyone is having a little rest.

Break time!
Rita and her friends build a snowman in
the playground.

'Miss! Someone's hit me
on the head with a snowball!'

'Children!' scolds the teacher.
'You really are impossible today!'

When Rita gets home, all she wants to
do is play with Whatsit.

'Come on, wake up, or I'll call you Limp Rag!'
'Too tired,' yawns Whatsit.

'But you haven't done anything all day,' cries Rita.
'Yes I have, I chewed your shoes…'

'And my half-chewed sweets?'
'I ate those too.'

'Whatsit! That's not allowed!'

Then it is bedtime.
'You know what?' says Rita. 'I've had an idea.
Tomorrow it's swimming at school. What if you
came too? I'll lend you my swimming cap.'

The only answer is a little snore.
Zzzzz.

A first day at school is tiring, even
for a dog with no name!

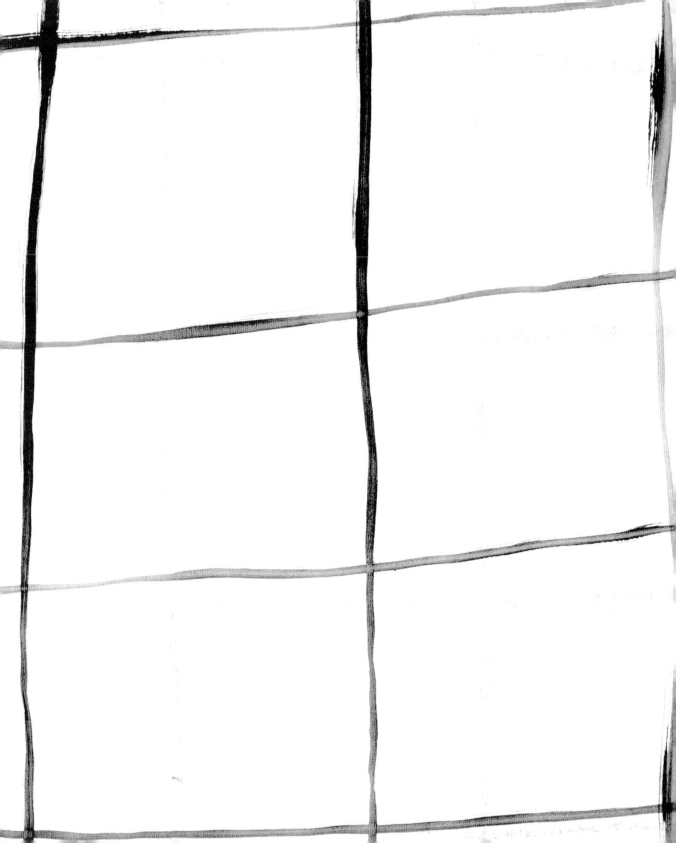

WESTERN ISLES LIBRARIES

RESOURCE CENTRE

Readers are requested to take great care of the item while in their possession, and to point out any defects that they may notice in them to the Librarian.

This item should be returned on or before the latest date stamped below, but an extension of the period of loan may be granted when desired.

J550

DATE OF RETURN	DATE OF RETURN	DATE OF RETURN
30 DEC 2016		
27 JUL 2018		
30 SEP 2023		